For Laura, whose words work wonders x – J.B.
For my dad, love you, and for CJ too xx – C.J-I.

First published 2017 by Macmillan Children's Books
an imprint of Pan Macmillan,
20 New Wharf Road, London N1 9RR
Associated companies throughout the world

www.panmacmillan.com

ISBN: 978-1-5098-3441-9 (HB)
ISBN: 978-1-5098-3442-6 (PB)

1 3 5 7 9 8 6 4 2

A CIP catalogue record for this book is available from the British Library.

Printed in China

With My Daddy

Written by
James Brown

Illustrated by
Cally Johnson-Isaacs

MACMILLAN CHILDREN'S BOOKS

Days with my daddy are always the best,
so full of adventures, there's no time to rest.
Together it's super, all giggles and fun,
because Daddy's so special, he's my Number One.

1
2
3

With Daddy it's breakfast time here at the zoo,
bananas for Teddy and strawberries for two.

"Explorers," says Daddy, "must kick-start their day.
Adventures are waiting, let's hop straight-away!"

What will we need to go out and about?
We both pack our bags and we leave nothing out.

With Daddy I buckle up quickly to race –
he counts us down fast as we blast into Space!

The park's an adventure, an island, a boat,
it's somewhere with treasure and somewhere remote.

My frisbee's a spacecraft way up in the sky,
and Daddy can launch it –

WHOOSH!

ever so high!

My daddy's a dancer,
he spins with a broom,

and glides with a vacuum
around every room.

His duster's a mic, and he sings like a pro,
he lets out a sneeze –

then it's on with the show.

Cooking with Daddy is always a treat,
his food is so tasty and such fun to eat.

Like magic, it's there when it's time for my tea
and it soon disappears . . .

in one,

two,

and three!

My daddy is super at sorting and sifting,

at tidying up

and heavy great lifting.

He finds missing pieces and hides things away

so everything's neat at the end of the day.

With Daddy the stairs spiral up to the sky
to a fairytale castle in clouds way up high.

We dodge past a dragon, a witch and a troll,
and save a lost princess, as sweet as a doll.

Then straight to the bath for a rub-a-dub-dub,
Captain Bubblebeard Dad makes me scrub-a-scrub-scrub!

Bath time is splash time when crabs nip my knees
and monsters blow bubbles and splash in the sea.

I love Daddy's stories, they're just like our day,
with fun things we've done, all the giggles and play.

He tucks me up tightly and kisses my head
then tickles the monster who's under my bed.

Daddy checks I'm all comfy and Teddy's alright,
then tiptoes on tiptoes to turn out the light.

"Close your eyes," he says gently, "and think what we'll do.
Tomorrow's adventures I'm sharing with you."

Days with my daddy are always the best,
they're full of adventures, but now I must rest.
I dream of tomorrow, more laughter and fun,
because Daddy's so special, he's my Number One.